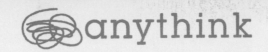

Everybody Feels...
JEALOUS

Moira Harvey
& Holly Sterling

Quarto is the authority on a wide range of topics.

Quarto educates, entertains and enriches the lives of our readers—enthusiasts and lovers of hands-on living. www.quartoknows.com

Author: Moira Harvey
Illustrator: Holly Sterling
Designer: Mike Henson
Editor: Carly Madden
Consultant: Cecilia Essau

© 2020 Quarto Publishing plc
This edition first published in 2020 by QEB Publishing,
an imprint of The Quarto Group.
26391 Crown Valley Parkway, Suite 220
Mission Viejo, CA 92691, USA
T: +1 949 380 7510
F: +1 949 380 7575
www.QuartoKnows.com

A CIP record for this book is available from the Library of Congress.

ISBN 978-0-7112-5019-2

Manufactured in Guangdong, China TT012020

9 8 7 6 5 4 3 2 1

Contents

Feeling jealous

Most people feel jealous sometimes.
You might get the feeling if...

...one of your
friends has a toy
that you want.

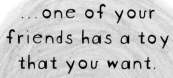

...your brother or
sister gets more
attention than you.

JEALOUS

...one of your
friends wins a prize
and you don't.

...somebody you
know gets more
praise than you.

...one of your
friends has been
given a treat that
you don't have.

How it feels

It's so unfair!

It isn't right!

You turn unkind.

Your mouth pulls tight.

Someone else got what you want

and now you're feeling...

Jealous!

Noah gets jealous

Hello. I'm Noah. I have a new baby brother named Joe. He's only small so he needs a lot of help and attention.

WAAAH!

Yesterday **I** wanted Mom to help me build a model. "I have to feed Joe," she said.

Then I asked Dad to read my book with me. "I need to change Joe's diaper," he said.

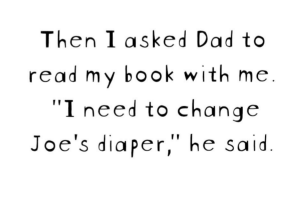

It was Joe this and Joe that.
Joe was getting everything.
It made me angry.
It made me feel jealous!

Argggh!

Then Mom began giving Joe a bath. It looked fun. Mom said I could help.

I dried Joe's tiny toes. He was as wriggly as a fish!

Tickle, tickle, Joe!

9

Dad tried to get Joe to sleep, and **I** thought of a way to help.

Twinkle, twinkle, little star.

I sang my best song and Joe fell asleep right away.

10

Mom and Dad both gave me a hug.
"We make a great family team," they said.

Thank you, Noah.

I didn't feel so jealous after
that. I was too busy being
Mom and Dad's top helper.

Ava gets jealous

Hello. I'm Ava. Yesterday I took
my robot Zoomie to the park.

My friend Noah was at the park, too.

He had a shiny new robot toy that was twice as big as mine.

Here comes Beepbeep, ruler of Robot Land!

I was jealous of Noah's toy.
I didn't want Zoomie any more.
I wanted Beepbeep.

I want a turn!

Let's play catching the bad guys!

14

I began to cry. Being jealous
made me feel unhappy and I
didn't want to play any more.

It's not fair!

"You could help me find the bad guys' base," said Noah. "It's under the chair. Beepbeep is too big to get in but Zoomie could try."

Zoomie is a hero!

Zoomie was small enough to get into the base. He saved us from the bad guys!

It didn't matter that Zoomie was smaller than Beepbeep. He was just as fun to play with. I didn't need to be jealous after all.

Here comes Beepbeep!

Here comes Zoomie!

Feeling better

Noah and Ava both made their
jealous feeling go away
by doing different things.

When Noah joined in looking after Joe, he stopped feeling jealous. He found out that he was very important to his Mom and Dad, and his brother, too.

Ava stopped feeling jealous of Noah's toy when she realized that her toy was good, too. They had fun playing with both toys.

Noah's story

1 Noah was jealous because his parents were so busy looking after his little brother. It made him feel angry.

2 Noah helped his Mom to bathe Joe. He was very helpful.

3 Then Noah sang Joe to sleep. He was really good at it.

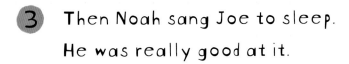

4 Noah realized that he didn't need to feel jealous after all. He was very important to his Mom and Dad and it was fun helping out with his little brother.

Ava's story

1 Ava took her robot toy, Zoomie, to the park.

2 Ava saw Noah's bigger robot, Beepbeep. She felt jealous and the feeling made her cry.

3 Ava's robot was the hero in a game of good guys v. bad guys.

4 Ava realized her toy was just as much fun to play with as Noah's toy. She stopped feeling jealous.

Story words

angry
When you get annoyed about something and perhaps even want to shout. Being jealous can make you feel that way.

attention
What you get when someone takes notice of you and talks to you.

feelings
When things that happen to you change the way you feel inside. Feelings can make you happy or unhappy.

helpful
When you do something kind and useful for someone. When you do this, like Noah did, it can chase jealousy away.

hero
A person who does something brave. You might play at being a hero in a game, like Ava did with her robot.

important

When you are important to someone they like you and want to be with you. Noah forgot he was important to his family, but he was.

joining in

Doing things with other people. Joining in can sometimes make you feel happy.

team

A group of people doing things together. Being on a team can be lots of fun.

thoughts

When you think about something. Being jealous can give you thoughts that will make you sad and upset.

unfair

When someone is treated wrongly. Sometimes the feeling of jealousy will make you think people are being unfair to you.

unhappy

A sad feeling that makes you cry.

unkind

Being horrible to someone. Jealousy might make you feel as if you want to be unkind.

Next steps

The stories in this book have been written to give children an introduction to feeling jealous through events that they are familiar with. Here are some ideas to help you explore the feelings from the story together.

Talking

- Discuss how Noah felt. He thought his parents didn't care about him as much as they cared about Joe. Was he right or wrong?
- Discuss how Ava felt. She wanted a toy that somebody else had, and thought her toy was worse. Was she right or wrong?
- Talk about how everyone sometimes gets their thoughts muddled, making them think things that aren't true. It happened to Noah and Ava.
- Look at page 4. Everybody is jealous sometimes. Talk about times when children might feel this way. Can your child think of times this has happened to them?
- Noah shouted and felt unkind when he felt jealous. Ava began to cry and thought everything was unfair. Ask your child how being jealous might make them behave.
- Look at the poem on page 5. You could help your child to write their own poem about what it's like to feel jealous.

Make up a story

On pages 20-21 the stories have been broken down into four-stage sequences. Use this as a model to work together, making a simple sequence of events about somebody feeling jealous and then feeling better. Ask your child to suggest the sequence of events and a way to resolve their story at the end.

An art session

Do a drawing session related to the feeling in this book. Here are some suggestions for drawings:

- A jealousy monster.
- The unhappy, angry face of someone feeling jealous.
- The happy face of someone who has realized they don't need to feel jealous.

An acting session

Choose a scene and act it out, for example:

- Role-play Noah and his Mom or Dad. Act out Noah feeling jealous, helping with Joe, and then being reminded how good and special he is.
- Role-play Ava and Noah in the park. Ava sees the big robot and gets jealous. Then she realizes her robot is good, too, and feels happy again.